W9-BGQ-753

My Favorite Foods

Written by Dana Meachen Rau
Illustrated by Grace Lin

Reading Advisers:

Gail Saunders-Smith, Ph.D., Reading Specialist

*Dr. Linda D. Labbo, Department of Reading Education,
College of Education, The University of Georgia*

LEVEL C

A COMPASS POINT
EARLY READER

For Mom and Dad

A Note to Parents

As you share this book with your child, you are showing your new reader what reading looks like and sounds like. You can read to your child anywhere—in a special area in your home, at the library, on the bus, or in the car. Your child will associate reading with the pleasure of being with you.

This book will introduce your young reader to many of the basic concepts, skills, and vocabulary necessary for successful reading. Talk through the details in each picture before you read. Then read the book to your child. As you read, point to each word, stopping to talk about what the words mean and the pictures show. Your child will begin to link the sounds of the letters with the look of the words that you and he or she read.

After your child is familiar with the story, let him or her read the story alone. Be careful to let the young reader make mistakes and correct them on his or her own. Be sure to praise the young reader's abilities. And, above all, have fun.

Gail Saunders-Smith, Ph.D.
Reading Specialist

Compass Point Books
3722 West 50th Street, #115
Minneapolis, MN 55410

Visit Compass Point Books on the Internet at *www.compasspointbooks.com* or e-mail your request to *custserv@compasspointbooks.com*

Library of Congress Cataloging-in-Publication Data

Rau, Dana Meachen, 1971–
    Favorite foods / by Dana Meachen Rau ; illustrated by Grace Lin.
        p. cm.
    Summary: A mother and child take a trip to the grocery store to buy all the child's favorite foods for a birthday party.
        ISBN 0-7565-0076-1 (hardcover : library bdg.)
        [1. Grocery shopping—Fiction. 2. Shopping—Fiction. 3. Food—Fiction. 4. Counting.]
I. Lin, Grace, ill. II. Title.
    PZ7.R193975 Fav 2001
    [E]—dc21   00-011848

What do we need
at the grocery store?

One scoop of juicy raisins.

1

One

Two heads of leafy lettuce.

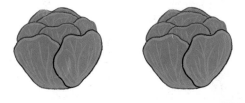

2

Two

Three jars of sticky jelly.

3

Three

Four cartons of chilly ice cream.

4

Four

Five cans of tasty soup.

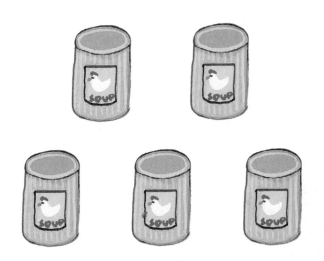

5

Five

Six tubs of spicy salsa.

6

Six

Seven bags of loopy noodles.

7

Seven

Eight packs of buttery popcorn.

8

Eight

Nine boxes of crunchy crackers.

9

Nine

Ten jugs of tangy juice.

10

Ten

The cart was so full!

The bags were so heavy!

We had a super birthday party
with all of my favorite foods!

More Fun with Foods!

Discuss with your child that everyone has different favorite foods. For example, the girl in this story did not have cake for her birthday. Instead she served all of the foods she loves: raisins, lettuce, jelly, ice cream, soup, salsa, noodles, popcorn, crackers, and juice. Tell your child your favorite foods. Ask him or her to make a list of his or her own favorite foods. See which foods you both like, and which foods are different.

The next time you and your child go to the grocery store, pretend you are on a scavenger hunt. This activity will teach your child observation and sorting skills. Encourage your child to find:

- things that are round
- things that are crunchy
- things that come in bags
- things that are pink
- things that go in the cabinet
- things that go in the refrigerator

Word List

(In this book: 66 words)

a	had	salsa
all	heads	scoop
at	heavy	seven
bags	ice	six
birthday	jars	so
boxes	jelly	soup
buttery	jugs	spicy
cans	juice	sticky
cart	juicy	store
cartons	leafy	super
chilly	lettuce	tangy
crackers	loopy	tasty
cream	my	ten
crunchy	need	the
do	nine	three
eight	noodles	tubs
favorite	of	two
five	one	was
foods	packs	we
four	party	were
full	popcorn	what
grocery	raisins	with

About the Author

Dana Meachen Rau loves to write and is the author of more than fifty books for children. She also likes to go grocery shopping. Her favorite aisle in the grocery store is the one with all the fruits and vegetables, because it is so colorful. Dana also loves oatmeal cookies, orange cheese, hot cocoa, and crunchy apples. Dana's husband, Chris, loves tacos, and their son, Charlie, loves bananas. They go shopping and make meals together in Farmington, Connecticut.

About the Illustrator

Grace Lin grew up in upstate New York and went to the Rhode Island School of Design. She now lives in Cambridge, Massachusetts, and is author and illustrator of the book *The Ugly Vegetables*, an ABA Pick of the List. Grace Lin's favorite food is ice cream. You can tell her your favorite food at *http://www.gracelin.com*.